and meet us all —

ANGUS & ROBERTSON PUBLISHERS

Unit 4, Eden Park, 31 Waterloo Road,
North Ryde, NSW, Australia 2113, and
16 Golden Square, London W1R 4BN,
United Kingdom

First published in Australia
by Angus & Robertson Publishers in 1977
Reprinted 1985, 1986, 1987

ISBN 0 207 13469 3

Printed in Singapore

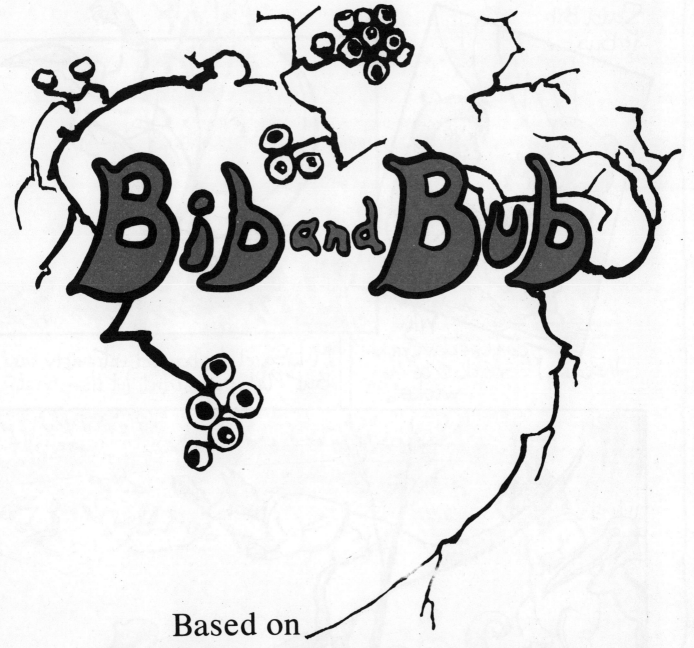

Bib and Bub

Based on
May Gibbs' original strip cartoons

Illustrated by Dan Russell

ANGUS & ROBERTSON PUBLISHERS

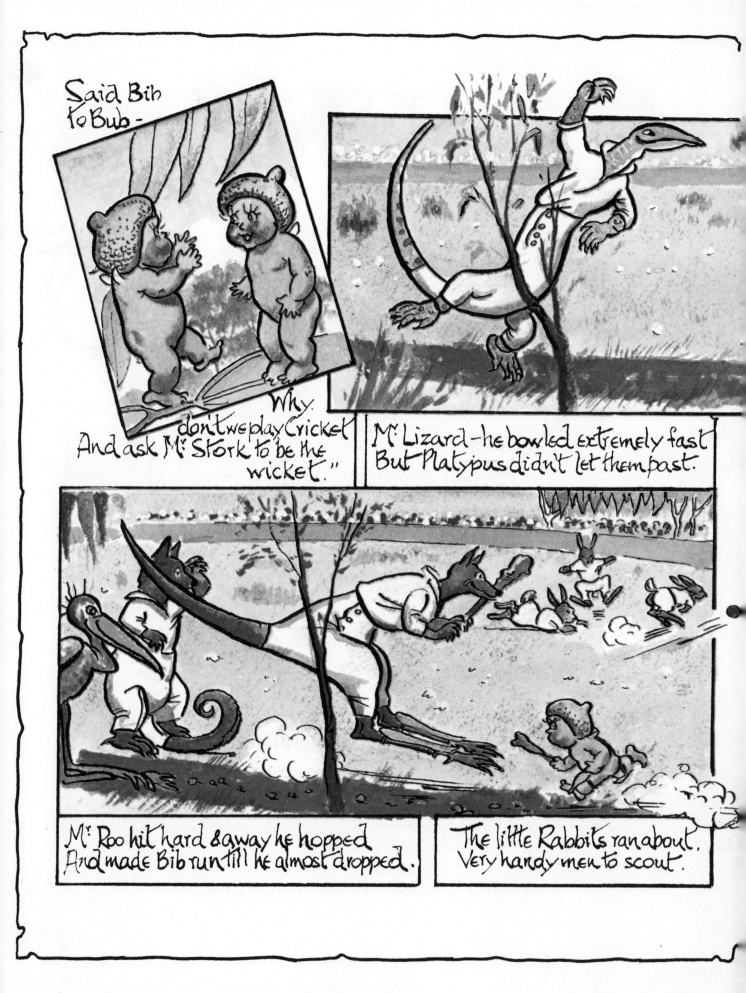

Mr Stork looked down his nose
He thought the ball might hurt his toes.

Mr Bear played strong & steady,
For Possum's googlies always ready

The crowd was large & very gay
Every one enjoyed the day.

But the game was spoilt. An Emu tall
Leaned over the fence & swallowed the ball.

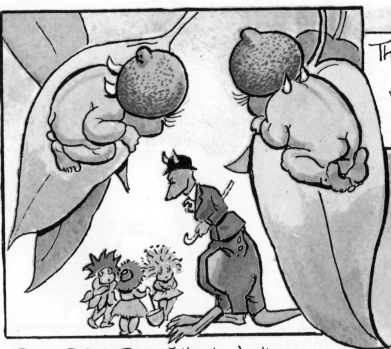

Said Bib to Bub "I think, don't you
"We ought to dress like Mr Roo?"

They asked advice of
Gran'pa Bear
Who only said
"Well I declare."

But Uncl
Cer

But when they met their friend
Mrs Bear

She passed them
with a haughty stare.

When they called at Mrs Cockatoo
door

She sat on
the step &
began to roar.

And Dr St
And shook

And so, with knocks &
grunts & care,
They made the very
ideal chair.

Mum Bunny liked it "Oh, so much".
She said "I'd love one in my Hutch."

"Oh bless my heart" cried
Mrs Bear
"What a perfectly lovely
little chair."

Then she sat down with such a bump,
And smashed the chair. car-rack-aly-ump.

ran down the street
met Mrs Bear,

Put out his tongue &
called her "Old Scare."

A little way on he passed Dr Stork.
He turned around & mimicked his walk

couldn't find anything better to do
he painted the tail of Miss. Kangaroo.

She caught him & beat him until he was red.
Oh, never get out on the wrong side of bed.

"I'm going to shop" said Mrs Bear.

But bye & bye He pulled quite well. Is many grateful friends could tell.

Said Bib & Bub "We'll take you there."

And when they did, I grieve to say,

Her buttons all had given way.

I'm told the poor thing cried with rage, The mending took her such an age.

Bib & Bub harnessed Stumpy
one day
And started off, some calls to
pay

First, they visited
Mrs Bear —

They had some tea & biscuits
there.

Next t
M^{rs} C

F.H.O

Then they called on Mummy Rabbit
And had more tea, through force of habbit.

Supper was on at Oposs
So of course they had to joi

called on
e ... Who gave them tea &
things again.

Then they dismounted at "The Log" ...
And had some tea with Mrs Frog. ...

Flat
that.

When they came to the
door of Dr Stork
They had grown so fat
they couldn't walk.

He gave them some tonic & put them to bed
So now they always take coffee instead.

Mrs Bear, she made a cake
And set it in the sun to bake.

She said, "Dear Nuts, will you be good,
And watch the cake?" They said they woul.

And hid behind a nearby tree
To find out what the fun would be.

But he no better vigil kept,
For very soon he also slept.

They meant
their faithful word to keep,
But very soon fell fast asleep.

Then Mr Lizard, jovial was
He put the cake into his bag.

Old Kookaburra, high in the air,
Had watched with glee the whole affair.

And shouting "Hi! Awake! Awake!"
Was just in time to save the Cake.

And all went very well —
until
They came to the foot of
a steep, steep
hill.

She took a party out one day
To picnic down at Sandy Bay

As it leapt
from the cliff, a gale
a   from the Sea
o

Carried it down to the top
of a tree.

And they might have been there to this very day,
But the Postman was passing & took
them away.